For Anaya, Roxy & Lily xxx—SGC
Wishing all children peace and safety.—AS

First American edition published in 2024 by

Crocodile Books
An imprint of Interlink Publishing Group, Inc.
46 Crosby Street
Northampton, Massachusetts 01060
www.interlinkbooks.com

Text copyright © Sital Gorasia Chapman, 2023
Illustrations copyright © Anastasia Suvorova, 2023

First published in Great Britain 2023 by Farshore
An imprint of HarperCollins*Publishers*, London

Library of Congress Cataloging-in-Publication Data available
ISBN 978-1-62371-678-3

1 2 3 4 5 6 7 8 9

Printed and bound in Malaysia

THE
BEDTIME BOAT

Sital Gorasia Chapman
Anastasia Suvorova

Crocodile Books, USA
An imprint of Interlink Publishing Group, Inc.
www.interlinkbooks.com

After so much **excitement** and fun,
Chandan's day was finally done.

A bath full of bubbles,

a brush of his teeth,

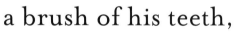

a big fluffy blanket
to cuddle beneath.

A favorite toy and a story to charm,
A softly sung song to make him feel calm.

"Sweet dreams my darling,"
Mom quietly said.

She hugged him
and kissed him
and tucked him
in bed.

Chandan looked cozy, all snuggled up tight.
But everything changed when
she turned out the light . . .

Dragons and dinosaurs whizzed around his head,
Rabbits and robots raced over the bed.

Alone in his room,
Chandan tossed and he turned.

He called out for Mom,
and Mom quickly returned.

"They won't let
me sleep!"
Chandan said,
looking glum.

So she placed the
bedtime boat
on his tum.

"Watch the boat, Chandan,
it floats on the ocean.

It rises and falls with your
breath's gentle motion."

Chandan tried hard to watch the boat sail,
But off in the distance he spotted . . .

. . . a whale.

It swam and it splashed
and was soon by his side.
He looked all around,
there was **nowhere** to hide.

It was the size of the moon
and the color of night,
It leapt overhead
and blocked out the light.

"It's going to crash!" cried Chandan in fright.
He covered his head and closed his eyes tight.

"Watch the boat, Chandan,
it floats on the ocean.

It rises and falls with your
breath's gentle motion."

Chandan watched the boat
float on the waves,

When off in the distance
he spotted . . .

. . . some caves.

They glittered and glimmered
with silver and gold,

Jewels of all colors
and riches untold.

His eyes grew wide and he laughed out in pleasure,
As he filled up his pockets with unguarded treasure.

A pirate ship's captain
crept up and screamed,

"STOP!"

Chandan jumped up
and let the loot drop.

The crew carried Chandan back to their ship:
"It's time for you to take a dip!"

"Watch the boat, Chandan,
it floats on the ocean.

It rises and falls with your
breath's gentle motion."

Chandan watched the boat
float in the dark,

Then found himself
eye to eye with . . .

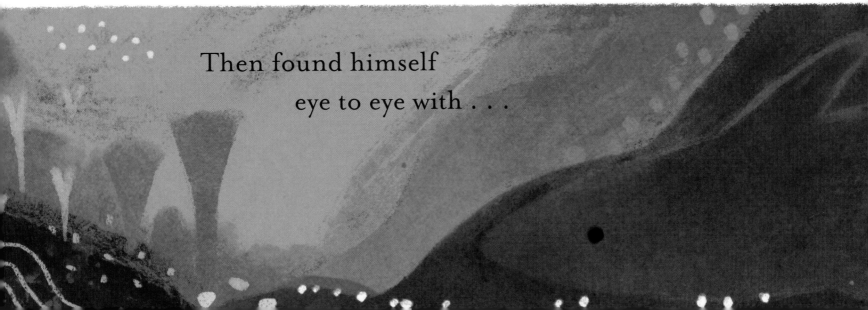

. . . A SHARK!

Its mouth full of teeth,
pointy and white.

Its jaws opened wide,
ready to bite.

Chandan trembled with fear
from his toes to his head.

And wished he was back
in the safety of bed.

"Watch the boat, Chandan, it floats on the ocean.
It rises and falls with your breath's gentle motion."

Chandan watched the boat fall and rise.
His breath grew slower; he rubbed his eyes.

He gazed at the stars dancing under the moon
As the wind whispered words to his favorite tune . . .

"Watch the boat, Chandan,
it floats on the ocean.
It rises and falls with
your breath's gentle motion."

He dropped the boat's anchor
to the sea floor,
And watched the tide gently
kissing the shore.

The waves' gentle whoosh
in the silvery light
rocked Chandan to sleep.

"Sweet dreams.
Good night."

MAKE YOUR OWN BEDTIME BOAT

In the story, Chandan watches his paper boat as it moves up and down with his breath. You can try it for yourself with any small toy or make your own paper boat (ask a grown-up to help you). Don't worry if your mind wanders, just try your best to bring your attention back to your breathing.

You will need a sheet of rectangular paper:

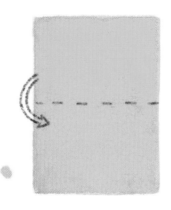

1. Fold it in half from top to bottom.

2. Then create a middle crease by folding the paper in half from left to right and re-opening.

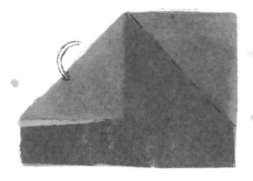

3. Fold the top corners down to the middle crease.

4. Fold the top layer of the bottom flap up, turn over and repeat on the other side.

5. Tuck the corners of each flap on the front under the flaps behind. Then fold over the flaps on the back so you can see them on the front.

6. Pull the sides of the pocket outwards from the middle crease, turn, then flatten into a diamond.

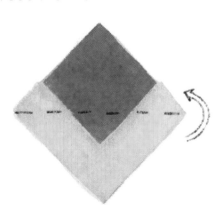

7. Fold the front layer in half from bottom to top, turn over and repeat on the other side to make a triangle.

8. Pull the sides of the pocket outwards from the middle crease, turn, then flatten once again.

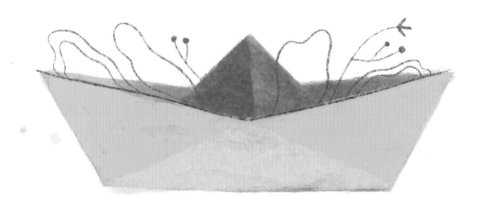

9. Gently open up the sides from the top to shape your boat.